$\mathcal{S}$ISTER $\mathcal{S}$HAKO
AND
$\mathcal{K}$OLO *the* $\mathcal{G}$OAT

Sister Shako
and
Kolo the Goat

MEMORIES OF MY CHILDHOOD IN TURKEY

BY VEDAT DALOKAY

TRANSLATED BY GÜNER ENER

LOTHROP, LEE & SHEPARD BOOKS
NEW YORK

Author's Note

*I*t was fifteen years ago, the first time I told the story of Sister Shako and Kolo the goat to my daughter Belosh. Sometime afterward I told it to my son Hakko, and later to Sibosh. Just recently I was about to tell it to Barish and Gözde, who had just reached their fifth and seventh birthdays, when I remembered that we were in the International Year of the Child. I thought that perhaps I might contribute a little bit to this important event by sharing with the children of the world this story of my childhood years.

When I was a small boy, I was very fond of sad stories and still am. I grew up. I developed a mustache and a beard — they even got white. I became an architect, I became a father, I became the mayor of the municipality of Ankara. But in all this time not much has changed. I have never been able to figure out when childhood stops, when a person becomes a "grown-up."

Each time my own children speak to me, they begin by addressing me as Father. The children in the street call me Uncle. But my mother, my wife, and especially my classmates say, "You are still a child." They are right; they tell the truth. I have never stopped being a child, not even for a moment!

VEDAT DALOKAY, ANKARA, TURKEY, 1979

Sister Shako's Hut

Because of a vendetta, they killed Sister Shako's husband and their two sons.

"Don't touch her," they said. "Take pity. She is the daughter of another family." So they left her alive.

Late one autumn, Sister Shako left her village, where she had been born, and grown up, and became her beloved Ali's bride, and given birth to their two sons. Except for her six goats, she had no one now.

She asked for shelter from my father, who was the landlord of our village.

My father gave her shelter in a deserted stable by the river. It was built of clay bricks. The first thing Sister Shako did was build a platform where she could place her bed and separate herself from the goats. With clay she fastened a piece of glass over a gap in the bricks where light came in. Next to that she built a beautiful fireplace, and over it a shelf. When I entered her hut for the first time, the latch of her door astonished me. It was a thick, strong stick, placed in a crevice in the wall, and could be opened from the inside as well as out, but it could not be opened by the goats. Not that Sister Shako had anything valuable to hide; the things she wanted to protect from the goats hung from the ceiling.

Here in this hut, Sister Shako slept and woke with her goats. During the summer, though, she let her goats sleep outside in front of the hut and laid her own bed on the roof. She was very much pleased with sleeping on the roof, "using all the stars of the sky as a quilt."

But I am getting ahead of myself . . .

How I Met
Sister Shako

*O*ne morning I was wading in the river in water up to my knees. I was looking for long, flat stones for my mother. She used them to break almond shells.

Suddenly someone grabbed my arm angrily and dragged me out of the water. "What the devil are you up to down there?" she yelled. "That river is full of Satan's Wells![1] She scolded me good and proper.

[1]Satan's Wells are dangerous holes in the bottom of a river.

I knew immediately that this must be Sister Shako, and for once I, the grandson of Landlord Mustafa, kept silent. But even though her eyebrows were frowning, her eyes were smiling, and they warmed my blood. I suddenly felt very close to her. Yes, and that was how I met Sister Shako.

It was Sister Shako's custom to turn her goats out with the common flock. Then she herself took the kids out to graze, so she was not always in sight during the day. That was why our meeting had been delayed. But I soon made up for the time we had wasted, and I became her closest friend. With her, my self-confidence grew, and I was very proud of our friendship, but I can't say that my father had the same feelings. He and my mother whispered about the situation, but thank goodness he did not forbid our friendship.

11

At first I was attracted to Sister Shako because of my appetite. Every morning, as soon as I woke up, I ran to her hut. She would spread a piece of sourdough bread, which she had baked on a metal sheet over the fire, with a slab of thick cream about the size of her hand, then slip it under a basket. I snatched and swallowed it in a minute.

Kolo the Newcomer

One evening not just six but seven goats came home to Sister Shako's hut. The newcomer was a huge female goat with bright yellow eyes and silky white hair.

"Oh, Great Creator, what a beautiful goat Kolo is!" said Sister Shako. "Is she not?"

"What does *kolo*[1] mean?" I asked.

---

[1]Kolo was the name of an ancient Khan (A.D. 552). Surely Shako knew nothing about him. For her, Kolo means something noble and magnificent.

"Look at her, she has no horns. She is special —
a kolo," Sister Shako explained. "She is not a goat of
this village; I wonder whose goat she is."

She washed her hands thoroughly, then milked
this goat that was a "Guest of God"[2] separately from
the others. Probably she meant to give the goat back,
together with its milk, if someone came to fetch it.

The next morning she thought that someone
would surely be waiting for his goat and that she
would not see it again, so she kissed its eyes when she
sent it to join the common flock. But that evening,
much to her surprise, Kolo returned to the hut.

Days and months passed, but no one asked about

[2]If a traveler needs shelter or food, he knocks at the door of any house
along his way. The host offers him whatever he needs, because the traveler
is considered a guest sent by God. This is a very old Turkish tradition that
is still practiced today.

Kolo. So Kolo came to belong to the hut, and she soon reigned over all the other goats — even the billy goat.

Kolo became Shako's favorite, the apple of her eye. She always held her tail straight up and her ears down. If Kolo's tail did hang down, Sister Shako ran immediately to gather the bulgur[3] she had laid out in the sun to dry, for she knew it would rain soon. If Kolo's ears pointed up, Sister Shako grew very cautious. "Either a wolf," she said, "or the gendarme sergeant is coming."

Sometimes, for a joke, Sister Shako hung her kerchief on the pointed end of Kolo's beard, which curved up like a hook. Then Sister Shako would kiss Kolo's eyes and call her "my sweet, coy Sultan."

[3]Bulgur is cracked wheat, the main dish of poor Turkish peasants.

The Pride of the Hut

$\mathcal{A}$lthough Kolo was a female goat, no billy goat was a better leader. Each evening when the flock returned from their mountain pasture, the first thing we saw from the village was a rising cloud of dust coming over the hill. Then Kolo's white hornless head emerged from the cloud, followed by hundreds of spearlike horns protruding from all-black heads. At the very end of the flock were the sheep.

Kolo stopped where the path turned off to the hut and waited for her own troop. Then she moved to her place at the back of the line and followed them home.

Sister Shako always milked Kolo first. If one of the other goats was milked before her, Kolo either tipped the bucket over or dropped her excrements into it like black olives falling from the holes of a worn-out sack. But even then, Shako never threw the milk away. She plunged her hand like a rake into the bucket and let the milk drain between her fingers, leaving Kolo's creations on her palm. Shako looked as if she felt like throwing them in Kolo's face, but instead she just cursed and threw them out the door. She soon learned that it was wiser to treat Kolo tactfully. Still, she knew from the beginning that that goat meant problems.

The evening that Shako went to cure the corporal's ailing wife with cupping glasses,[1] one of her friends milked the goats, but he could not find a way to milk Kolo. He forced her to stand still and squeezed her teats until they turned purple, but he could not get even one drop of milk from her full udder. Around midnight, when Shako returned, she washed her hands, then kissed Kolo's eyes. After that Kolo relaxed and allowed herself to be milked.

Kolo's udder was the pride of the hut, and nothing bad could be said about it. The hand that milked her was never again a stranger's hand, nor was it ever a dirty hand.

[1]Cupping glasses are an old way of curing the ill by placing glass cups over the area in pain, thus creating a kind of vacuum.

The Black Snake

*O*ne afternoon near sunset I heard my father
calling me, "Run quickly, my son, and
bring my rifle!"

I carried the rifle to the old mulberry tree, where
my father was waiting for me. The branches of the
tree were loaded with sparrows, a flurry of fluttering
wings. My father aimed at the lowest branch and
pulled the trigger.

It felt like doomsday. The air was filled with

19

smoke and the smell of gunpowder. Hundreds of sparrows took off and disappeared. A deep silence fell over everything. Then a big black snake slid down the trunk — in two pieces.

The peasants gathered around. They removed two dead sparrow chicks from the plump stomach of the snake. Sister Shako took the chicks, and the peasants took the snake. They buried it under the barren walnut tree in the remotest part of the garden.

"The tail of the snake will not die unless it sees the stars," said one of the peasants. Another turned to me. "Little Lord, you must never pass by here barefooted. If a bone of the snake enters your foot, you will limp like Crippled Hasso.

Later on, all the peasants gathered and knelt down around my father, who was sitting under the pear tree. Each told a story about his own experience with a snake. Finally one said, "Lord, the mate of the snake will surely come tonight to take revenge, to harm one of us. We must be all eyes and ears for our children and women."

That night I could not sleep a wink. At every little sound I sprang out of bed and searched everywhere. I longed for dawn.

In the morning, as soon as the sun was born, I ran to Shako's hut. "Sister Shako," I asked, "what did you do with the dead sparrows? Where did you bury them?"

"I used them to cast a magic spell over the hut," she told me. "I cleaned them with milk and wrapped them in gauze and hung them over the fireplace. Here they are."

"What happened to the snake's mate? Where do you think it went?"

"It was here," said Sister Shako. "When I woke up at dawn and looked around, the dragon was sleeping coiled up on the edge of my cushion."

"What!" I cried. "What did you do then? Did you kill it?"

"It had not touched me, dearest," she told me, "so I did not touch it either."

Questions

Sister Shako's attitude toward the snake caused a great question in my mind. She was always relaxed around scorpions, mole-crickets, hornets, and wasps — things that scared me to death. After a rain or on very warm evenings, the walls of her hut were covered with lizards and scorpions, but she never bothered about them. She killed a scorpion only if it intended to sting her.

Neither was she afraid of dead people, or of dying

herself. For her, to die was "a way to continue life." Yet it seemed to me that she took life so seriously and clung to it in such a way that there could be no death for Sister Shako.

One day when I entered the hut, my eyes were slow to get accustomed to the darkness. I didn't see the bucket filled with fresh milk, and I tipped it over. The sweet-smelling milk spilled out over the dirt floor and slowly sank into the earth.

"Don't worry, dearest. These things just happen," said Sister Shako. "One day you and I will be mixed with the earth exactly like this. I pray to the Creator that your time will be long in coming, but I can't hang on much longer. Here in my chest I had a great pain last night. Now I can't control my hands and feet properly."

"Are you ill, Shako?"

"Yes, dearest."

In her old, full dress, Shako seemed like a dried branch. She caught my hand and pressed it under her ribs.

"Here," she said. "Right here."

I ran home and told the news to my mother, who picked something up and went away. When she returned, she told me, "Very early tomorrow, your father will go hunting. Sister Shako is ill. Tomorrow you must take the kids to the riverside. Be careful to keep them out of the village."

That night I could not sleep. I kept seeing Sister Shako's dried, skinny body. I kept thinking that when she had pressed my hand on her ribs, I had not felt her ribs but her soul.

At last the sun rose. The cocks were crowing; the dogs were barking. My father went down to the stable, and soon after I saw his head and his horse's head passing behind the hedge.

I rushed down to Sister Shako's hut. She was already awake. To my relief, the color of her face looked better.

That day I took Kolo's two all-white kids and the four all-black kids of the other goats to the pasture by the river. It was a beautiful day, one of the most beautiful I can remember. Before sunset we paraded back to the hut, the kids in front, their bellies bulging out like balloons, with me following them proudly like a king.

The flock had not yet returned, but, surprisingly, Kolo was in the hut, standing quietly near Shako, who was lying on her bed.

"Is it you, dearest?"

"Yes."

"Help me milk Kolo."

I turned Kolo's teats toward the bed and pushed the bucket under her udder, which was swollen so tight with milk it hardly fit between her legs. Then I fetched water so Sister Shako could wash her hands. She turned on one side and caught hold of Kolo's teats. The milk sprayed out like threads, *fsh fsh,* until it filled the whole big bucket to the brim. Sister Shako looked at it in astonishment and murmured, "I swear, dearest, I have never seen anything like this in my entire life."

Malaria

When I got home that evening, my cheeks were red and my shirt was soaked with sweat. Mother, who was always afraid that I would catch malaria, stripped me and rubbed and dried my body thoroughly. She made me swallow a bitter quinine tablet together with some hot linden flower tea, then put me to bed under a big, thick quilt. I was burning hot, but still I shivered with cold and my teeth chattered. When I slept, my dreams were filled with Kolo questions: Why had she returned early? Had she sensed that Sister Shako was ill? How had she found her way? And where did all that milk come from?

I awoke suffocating with fever. My bed was drenched with sweat. Mother dried me, dressed me in fresh underwear, and put me into another bed. I fell asleep once more and dreamed that I was with the kids in the pasture by the Crazy River.

When I awoke again, it was midday. My mind was still full of questions.

"All night long, you talked in your sleep, my son," my mother told me.

"Is Sister Shako well, Mother?"

"She has already gone to the riverside with the kids. She left your cream here when she passed by."

I was ill for some time, and throughout my illness all my dreams were about Kolo and the kids. I had seen Kolo in many moods — stubborn, proud, loving, angry — and I had seen her kids playing their incredible games, but still, questions continued to fill my mind.

Kolo's Revenge

*L*ate one afternoon after I had recovered, I was drinking water from Stone Spring. Kolo's thirsty kids were at the spring too, but upstream from me. As they drank, they stirred up the mud at the bottom with their hooves, so the water running toward me turned muddy. They looked shocked when I cracked their bottoms with a thorny oleaster branch, those naughty little ones.

The next day it was my turn to be shocked. The

mulberries I had picked were scattered all over the place, the flutes and whistles I had made of elder-berry branches and spread on the roof to dry were all on the ground and broken, and that evening Kolo struck a hornets' nest with her round belly so that it fell right in front of me. I barely escaped the angry hornets. I had no doubt that she and her little kolos did all these things on purpose, and I explained this to Sister Shako.

"When the hair of a rose hip gets into someone's neck, it makes him jump like a donkey stung by a hornet," Sister Shako said. "Kolo and her kids are like rose hip hair when they are angry."

The Creator and Shako

fter the evening when Sister Shako had been ill and Kolo had given a big bucketful of milk, the amount of Kolo's milk dwindled to half; she began to yield milk just as before. This made Sister Shako cross.

"The evil eye has turned on Kolo, dearest," she said. "Tomorrow when the sun is highest, we shall go to Sultan Hidir."[1]

[1] Sultan Hidir was a regional saint whose grave was under the Purple Rock.

The next day at noon I went to the hut. Shako was waiting for me, her sack already hung from her shoulder. We set out on our journey. We were going to Purple Rock to make a vow.

We reached a gorge between two mountains, and there it stood, high and purple. It was holding a juniper tree down as if to crush it, but there was no holding it down. Stubbornly, the tree had sprung out on all sides from under the rock.

The juniper tree, decorated with thousands of rags bound to its branches, looked like a strange camel. Sister Shako murmured something and tied one of her old kerchiefs to a branch.[2] Afterward, as if her

[2]There are some holy places in Turkey where people go to pray and seek fulfillment of their wishes. When they leave, they bind a piece of cloth to anything around to signify that they have been there. Thus these places of prayer are covered with scraps of clothing.

palms were full of water, she stroked her face.

She took fresh white cheese, green onions, and sourdough bread out of her sack. We had a nice meal, then drank some ice cold water before we started back.

"What did you say, Shako, while you were tying your kerchief to the tree?" I asked her.

"I called out to the Creator, dearest."

"Did the Creator hear you? Was Father God there?"

Sister Shako started. She looked into my eyes. Probably my question surprised her.

Then she went to the nearest melon garden and picked a melon. When she came back, she struck the melon against a stone. She pointed to the seeds that fell from the melon as it broke.

"Now, tell me, dearest, if God is not here, then who put all these holy seeds inside of this melon?"

The Imam's Rosary

*A*fter we returned from Sultan Hidir, we kept an eye on Kolo, but her milk lessened with each day. We were happy that Sister Shako's illness was over, but we were bothered by the matter of the milk. At last Sister Shako said, "Just this once, let's try going to Pilgrim-Imam of our village."

We took a gauze sack filled with fresh cheese with us. And we brought Kolo, who had been affected by the evil eye, to the Iman.[1] But as soon as Kolo caught sight of the holy man (or perhaps it was his magnificent beard), she got very upset. Her tail turned downward; her ears shot straight up. She spread her legs and properly washed the very small inner courtyard of the Imam's house with her urine. The Imam, murmuring a prayer to calm himself, fumbled for his rosary, which he had placed at his side, but he could not find it.

"This goat is stricken by the goblins!" he roared in anger. "Now get out of here!"

We packed up our belongings and set out for the hut. I was really embarrassed. Sometimes I could not understand Sister Shako's affairs.

That same evening Kolo got some horrible pains.

[1]An Imam is the leader in public worship, a kind of Muslim priest.

Kolo, who usually never moved her beard, not even while chewing her cud, began to toss her head left and right, and she groaned all through the night. Shako thought that Kolo was "captured by blood,"[2] so she bled the goat by cutting a slit in her ear.

In the morning, Shako could not squeeze one drop of milk out of Kolo, but she counted exactly thirty-three yellow amber beads as they fell from Kolo's popo, *plop plop,* into the milk bucket. Both Kolo and Sister Shako took a deep breath of relief.

I arrived to fetch my thick cream just in time to see Shako putting the beads on a string and the Imam's rosary gradually reappearing. When it was complete, Shako rubbed it on Kolo's beard.[3] Then

[2]To be "captured by blood" means to have high blood pressure.
[3]It is a Turkish custom to rub an unexpected gift on your beard before accepting it

she asked me to hang it with my lucky hand[4] from the best spot on the ceiling.

"Don't say a word about this to anyone," she told me. "Hold your tongue." She hesitated for a moment, then, thinking she had better explain, she continued, "You must always be master of your tongue, your hands, and your body, dearest."

[4]A person considered to have been born lucky is said to have a lucky hand. The author was born lucky to be the son of the landlord.

Father Munzer

*B*arely two days later, Kolo baffled Sister Shako once again, this time by giving two buckets of rich blue-white milk, loaded with the scents of thyme and rose geranium. But instead of being pleased, Shako turned pale. She knelt down and touched her forehead to the earth.

"I beseech you, be quiet," she told me. "Our Kolo, like Father Munzer, has probably become a saint."

Then she told me about Father Munzer, a young man who had once seemed like an ordinary shepherd. As she told the story, she got very excited. She stood up, waving her arms and speaking louder and louder, each word clear and distinct.

"Oh, dearest, at the end, the peasants realized that shepherd Munzer had turned into Saint Munzer. His face now shone with divine light, and they ran to kiss his hand and skirt. But Father Munzer, who was unaware of what was happening, grew frightened by the screaming, pushing peasants. Holding the bowl of milk from which he had drunk in his hand, he backed away from them. Milk splashed from his bowl, and wherever a drop fell, the rocks cracked, and out of each of them arose a spring. Forty springs arose, I beseech you to believe me, forty springs! Then, just as the peasants were about to touch him, the rocks cracked and Father Munzer vanished. A miracle! Forty drops of milk turned into forty springs and ran as forty streams. Forty streams embraced one another and turned into the Crazy Munzer River!"

Exhausted, Sister Shako knelt down on the earth. "I would sacrifice my life for God who created the Crazy Munzer River out of milk drops," she said.

As if she were chasing away some invisible things, she moved her head and hands from side to side and spat in both directions. Then she rubbed her lips with the back of her hand and remained silent.

Kolo's Teats

*O*ur neighbor Mr. Asim named the grape-vine in his yard that yielded the best fruit "Kolo's teats." One day he picked a basketful of grapes and sent them to my father. I was fascinated by their name. They really *were* like Kolo's teats: plump and long at the same time, with hard red tops.

That evening I brought my share of grapes to Sister Shako. "Take a good look at them," I told her.

43

"These grapes are called 'Kolo's teats.'" And I went on joking about them for some time.

The next morning I saw Mr. Asim running madly from one end of the village to the other, tearing his hair and beard in fury. "I'll find that devil!" he kept shouting. His grapevine, his pride and joy, had been bitten off at the root.

Kolo's Territory

he place in the hut where Kolo slept was like Sister Shako's place: high and very clean. No one had ever seen Kolo drop excrements or piss where she slept. Once a year, for just one evening, she moved and slept next to the billy goat, whose sour smell she found irresistible, but they did not mate on that evening; she only wanted to calm him down and make peace with him. For a week or ten days afterward, she grazed with him and went to the spring with him — until he became quite content and she was with twins, little kolos. While the other goats of the hut gave birth to only one kid, Kolo *always* had twins. One of them was a girl, Kolofosh; the other was a boy, Kololo.

When the kids were born, Kolo suckled them at home. She played, grazed, and went to the river with them; she licked their coats and taught them how to lick themselves, how to catch fleas, and how to smash ticks. In short, she tried to teach them everything she knew.

One evening as she washed the muddy hooves of the little kolos, Sister Shako said, "Today Kolo probably taught them the lesson of the mole-cricket. If a mole-cricket hidden in the grass stings their noses while they are grazing, not only a goat but even a cow will collapse on the spot."

As autumn drew to a close, Kolo stopped going to graze with the flock. Her milk was drying up, her mouth was parched, and her eyes were filled with tears. Sister Shako immediately understood what was the matter. At the end of autumn, when Kolo saw the wheat sprouting green leaves and the mountain ash berries turning red, she knew that the day of separation from her little kolos would soon arrive. She acted as if a knife had been stuck into her heart. She seemed to know that Sister Shako would soon take all the kids, including her little kolos, to the marketplace and sell them.

Sister Shako had no choice. She did not have enough hay for more than seven goats. And she had a lot of shopping to do to prepare for winter.

Those days were hard and filled with sorrow. Both

47

Shako's and Kolo's hearts burned secretly. One of them understood the consequences of being poor; the other understood a goat's destiny. It was the law of nature, but each had the heart of a mother and they were helpless.

The Gendarmes

*E*arly one afternoon, lots of gendarmes came to the village. "They say they are hunting either bandits or deserters," said Sister Shako, "but these are just idle excuses for a mean sergeant to make us suffer."

The gendarmes camped on the pasture by the river, where the kids always went to graze. Their tents looked like two white pixie hats. Sister Shako had been upset since morning when she milked Kolo and

49

noticed her tail turned downward, and she became gloomier as the day wore on. In the evening when she saw all the kids return to the hut except Kololo, she immediately understood what had happened and her knees gave way.

The two of us went outside in front of the hut and stood staring at the tents. The gendarmes were sitting in a circle around a huge fire, which was burning down into hot red cinders. In the middle of the fire . . . oh, no, no! Neither Shako nor I could bring ourselves to say it.

Crying, clenching my fists in anger, I started home. Down by the river, I saw the gendarmes singing and dancing joyfully. Stuffing themselves with grilled Kololo, they sang and danced wildly until midnight.

But when they went to sleep, their stomachs began to rumble. The gendarmes, stricken with a merciless diarrhea, left their tents one by one, rushing first to the ditch, then to the river to wash. Soon they were rushing in a flock, first to the ditch, then to the river, on and on and on until morning.

By sunrise, when I was on my way back to Sister Shako's hut, the grass, the rocks, and the brambleberry bushes by the river were covered with underpants that had been washed and left to dry. The scene looked like the holy juniper tree at Purple Rock.

"What's going on, Sister Shako?" I asked.

In an angry, hoarse voice, she replied, "I pray the gendarmes will burst!"

Dried Dung and Bread

In front of the hut, Sister Shako, her sleeves rolled up, was kneading mud mixed with big pieces of straw. I was excited because I thought she was going to repair the hut or build a small addition and I wanted to help.

"You better stand aside, dearest," she told me. "You are not suited for this."

As she sat there in a cloud of tiny flies and ugly smells, I realized that she was not kneading mud, she was kneading manure. Then I remembered how, lately, she had been putting a basket on her back and following the herd of cattle on their way back to the village in the evenings. And how yesterday she had brought her goats' pellets to Corporal Memet's garden and exchanged them for baskets full of cow dung from the corporal's stable. Now I understood that all this activity had been in preparation for today's work.

Her work reached its peak when Sister Shako set out huge heaps of the kneaded mixture and formed them like loaves of bread. One by one she pasted them carefully on the sunny wall of the hut.

"Now this work is done, dearest," she said. "These are needed for the hard winter."[1]

[1]In the villages of eastern Turkey, dried dung is used as a kind of fuel to burn in fireplaces and heat houses in winter.

Then she went down to the river, cleaned herself properly, and returned. She checked her creations, which were blooming like high roses on the wall. Then she went into the hut, fetched her pastry board, her rolling sticks, and the flour sack, and placed the oven sheet on the fireplace outside the hut. All day her skilled hands had decorated the walls of the hut with magnificent dried dung; now in the early evening they plunged into bread dough.

The sun had set. The dusty cloud of the flock returning to the village was still behind the hill, but the full udders would reach the hut soon, and Sister Shako's hands would turn to the last task of the day.

Shako and Life

Sister Shako used to take a jug full of Kolo's fresh milk to each young bride in the village just before her wedding. She stripped the girl and rubbed her naked body thoroughly with Kolo's milk, and she recommended to the bride that she offer the rest of the milk to the groom on their wedding night.

Sister Shako also made a stonelike cheese from Kolo's milk, left it to dry under the sun, then put it in a thin cloth sack and hung it from the ceiling of her hut. Whenever it was needed, she took a clod of the cheese, smashed it in a glass of water, and gave it to children who had stomachaches. As soon as they drank it, their stomachaches went away and their stools turned hard as bricks!

No illness could remain if touched by Sister Shako's hand and Kolo's milk. Yet Sister Shako could not find a remedy for herself. She knew that there was none to be found.

"It is different, my illness, dearest, quite different," she told me. "It is like the tobacco weed growing at the foot of the cucumber plant. Even if you get rid of the weed, the cucumber plant will still dry up. My trouble is like this, dearest. It keeps gnawing at something inside of me . . . I cannot hang on much longer."

When she saw that I was deeply saddened, she wanted to comfort and give me strength.

"Dearest, it is the will of our Creator. When I die, I know it will take less than a year for me to become a handkerchiefful of soil, and I shall be one with the field and the water. Through them I shall be the sap rising in the heads of the wheat, I shall be the blossoms on an almond branch, I shall be the scent of oleaster flowers. I shall be the grass in the pasture and I shall be the milk in Kolo's udder. Look, exactly like this in the bucket. I shall enter the blood of whoever drinks Kolo's milk, and I shall be in your flesh, in your bones, in the light of your eyes, dearest."

She spoke as if she were singing a song — the song of her beloved Ali. I understood there was no boundary between Sister Shako and death; one was absorbed by the other. Like water soaked up by the field and evaporating in the sky, like a green almond hardening into a mature almond, like the sun setting only to rise again, death was the beginning of a new life.

"Now I am here in this hut; but after death I shall be in the caterpillar on the black earth, I shall be in the rain seeping into the earth. Blowing winds and rapid rivers will carry me all around this world. May death come nicely, smoothly, without pain, without suffering."

Sister Shako and
the Landlord

ister Shako had laid Kolo on her side in
front of the hut and bound her four legs
together to a stick. She was cutting Kolo's long hair
with a rough pair of shears when I arrived.

"Come, dearest, I am going to knit a pair of socks
for you with this hair," she said. Then she went on
cutting, *chop chop*. She piled the tufts of long silky
hair in front of me, saying,

"Look, this is the good landlord."

Where the hair was cut, I could see ticks stuck to Kolo's skin. Shako pulled the ticks, which had sucked Kolo's blood and turned into hard nuts, off the goat's skin. She smashed them under her foot, saying,

"Look, these are the bad landlords."

When she finished her work, before she took Kolo to the river to wash her, she explained what she meant. "The good landlord brings us prosperity, and the bad landlord brings us poverty, dearest."

Since a Flock of Sheep Cannot Fly Like Birds...

When the shepherd was called to military service, a new one came to take care of the village flock. This new shepherd knew nothing about Kolo, and he was soon very annoyed with this crazy goat who was always at the peak of the mountain or on top of a rock as steep as a wall. One day the new shepherd took a big sling and hurled a rock at the unruly goat, who had once again broken loose from the flock. The huge stone whirred through the air and fell to the ground just a foot away from Kolo, where it broke into small pieces. Deep in her nostrils Kolo must have smelled the warm smoke coming from the sparks of shattered stone and been scared to death.

The next afternoon, when the shepherd woke up after a nap in an oak tree, the whole flock was over on the other side of the river. The shepherd, who seemed stricken by goblins, raced back to the village, screaming and yelling. All the villagers rose to their feet — the old ones, the young ones, the girls, the children, the mothers, the fathers. Carrying tree trunks, timber, coils of rope, inflated boats, and hollow water-pumpkins, they reached the riverside. Not until evening did they manage to move the flock back across the river.

I was not in the village that day. My father had taken me to the city to be photographed and to be vaccinated against smallpox, because I was about to begin secondary school. But that evening, everybody was talking about the events of the day. I ran to Sister Shako's. She was joyfully stirring something in a pot in front of the hut. It meant that we would eat bulgur.

"Is it possible, Sister Shako, that such a thing can happen? Did that flock turn into birds and fly to the other side of the river?"

"Listen to me, dearest. I can no longer count how many years have passed since it happened. It was a long time ago. The landlord of our village said no, so my parents would not let me marry my Alosh.[1] One

[1] Alosh is an affectionate nickname for Ali.

pitch dark night I ran away from home to join him. We were going to hide ourselves in his uncle's place on the other side of the river. It was the beginning of May, when the river was in it craziest mood, roaring as it ran. In blind darkness we stripped. My Alosh made a bundle of our clothing and his rifle and bound it on the top of his head; then he bound one end of his sash around my waist and the other to his arm. We waded into the water at the bend where the current was strongest, then let ourselves be carried by the crazy river that looked like a dragon under the light of the stars."

"Did you know how to swim, Sister Shako?"

"Nay. My Alosh said that he would take care of me. I left myself to him. The current snatched us quickly and carried us for some distance. Once the river pulled me down, but Alosh pulled me up again to the surface with the sash bound to his arm. Later, at another bend, the river tossed us up on the opposite bank. There it left us like sand.

"We did not go to the uncle's place; we stayed in the mountains. When I woke up in the morning, my Alosh was picking wild violets . . ."

Sister Shako bowed her head as if she were smelling the purple violets and remained silent. She played with the corner of her kerchief, and I am sure I know what she wanted to say: "Whatever Kolo does, the village flock does too; they follow her. Do you think that Kolo wasn't smart enough to know what my Alosh knew?" But she could not say it, for she was sad and lost in thought and still in love with her Alosh.

Without saying a word I left quietly, with Sister Shako's favorite song in my ears:

In the morning at sunrise
I saw Ali, my Ali,
I placed my head on his knee,
I saw Ali, my Ali.

The Fleas of
the Corporal

When early autumn arrived, Sister Shako boiled bulgur and made töpür.[1] During that time she did not pay much attention to the kids.

The kids' favorite spot was the corporal's sour cherry orchard, as if there were no other good places around and not a pinch of grass left. One day, after six kids had gnawed all the foliage off the sour cherry trees and ruined the garden, the corporal came run-

[1]Töpür is the starch made of boiled bulgur.

ning, but it was too late. He penned the kids in his dark and dirty stable and made straight for Sister Shako's hut.

The corporal's anger was so great that Sister Shako barely saved her life. He helped himself to her skin bag of cheese as compensation for the damage and carried it home under his arm. Then he let the kids out of the stable.

I heard the corporal's loud voice — clearly he had never caught malaria[2] — and I ran to the hut. By the time I arrived, the fight was over and the corporal had already left. A little later, all the kids except one, which had been kept as a hostage, returned to the hut.

Sister Shako was furious. She threw the kids,

[2]"He never caught malaria" is a colloquial saying meaning that he has a strong, healthy voice.

covered with thousands of fleas from the corporal's filthy stable, out of the hut. As she drove them to the pasture by the river, she cursed loudly with every step. Between curses she said to me, "Dearest, we've got some urgent business to do. You better come early tomorrow to fetch your thick cream."

So I was dismissed too.

Before sunrise I was back at the hut. We drove six goats and five kids down to the riverside. There we tied a tuft of goat hair to the ears of each kid and the horns of each goat. Then, in a peaceful bay made by a deep bend in the river, we went into the water, Sister Shako and Kolo in front, the kids and I at the back. We moved forward slowly until the water reached the goats' horns and the kids' ears. When only the tufts of hair were above water, we hurriedly untied the tufts and set them adrift. Sister Shako took care of the goats and I the kids. Then we stood and watched the tufts of goat hair, each covered with thousands of fleas terrified of the water, float down the crazy, cold river to conquer someone else's stables.

The Billy Goat and
the Cruel Wolf

*O*ne ill-omened evening, Kolo entered the hut before the others. Sister Shako observed her carefully. Her tail hung downward and her eyes were full of pain. She looked as if she were bringing bad news, and she was. The billy goat was missing. Sister Shako went out of the hut to search for him. Then she saw me.

"Dearest, the billy goat did not return with the flock," she told me.

After a while, the shepherd appeared in the distance, walking toward us, carrying a goat skin on his back. He placed the bloody hide in front of Shako.

"The wolves attacked the flock, Sister Shako," he said. "Some sheep and also your billy goat . . . . First the dogs ran off, and then I followed them, but the billy goat was already on the ground. He was still twitching when I managed to reach him with my knife, so your billy goat did not die unclean.[1] Here are his skin and the best parts of his flesh. God save you, Shako," he said, and left soon after.

While the shepherd was telling all this, I was frozen to the spot. Ordinarily I refused to believe in tales of dramatic and bloody events, but here was the

[1]According to Islamic rule, animals must be slaughtered with a knife. Otherwise they will be considered "unclean" or "uneatable."

blood-stained hide lying before my eyes. They filled with tears. Suddenly I could see how the billy goat and the wolf had fought. The billy goat was defending himself well against the wolf, who was attacking from the front; he didn't want to leave his Kolo a widow yet. Bravely he resisted the cruel and cowardly enemy, fighting till the end. But what could he do when another wolf attacked him from behind? He was forced to deliver himself and his soul to his enemy.

Sister Shako wiped away her tears. She combed my hair with her fingers and said, "Dearest, look, Kolo is pregnant again. The kids of the billy goat are there. He is gone, that is all . . ."

But I knew that life for Shako and Kolo would be harder than before.

The Death of
Sister Shako

*W*hen the hard winter, with its lunar eclipse and its bitter cold, was nearly over, the pain in the right side of Sister Shako's chest started again. It lasted quite a long time.

The first signs of spring appeared, the cold broke, and snowdrops drilled up through the snow with the good news of approaching spring. Then the pain struck Shako on the left side. She was despondent and grieved, "I have no hope left anymore, dearest. It is God's will."

One morning while I was on my way to fetch my thick cream, I felt as if a black snake were coiling up inside of me. In the darkness of the hut, the first thing I saw were Kolo's yellow eyes filled with pain, then Sister Shako's peaceful, yellow face. She did not turn to look at me. I approached her bed and saw that her feet were sticking out from under the quilt. I wanted to push them back under the covers, but when I touched them, they were ice cold and hardened. A cold, thorny shiver ran down my back; a great fear came over me. I felt like I was suffocating, and I ran to my mother.

Mother told me to stay at home. She gathered everyone in the household and together they ran to the hut. Soon my mother returned.

"We have lost Sister Shako, my son. Last night she died."

Suddenly I could hear the chirrups of the sparrow chicks waking up on the grapevine by the fountain pool. I buried my face in the sofa cushion and cried.

Have You Seen the Kolos?

Not until afternoon did my mother allow me to go out. The peasants were returning from the cemetery, carrying spades and diggers in their hands. Leading the way were the corporal and the bearded Imam.

I went to the cemetery. Between the canal and a squat juniper tree was a fresh heap of earth and an uncarved white stone. I felt as though Shako's peaceful, sweet voice were mixing with the roar of water running in the canal at her side.

I shall go on living in the yellow heads of wheat, dearest; I shall dissolve in the blue-white milk; I shall be the greening in the almond tree that you planted; I shall be in the light in your eye . . . . I shall be heard in the call of the red partridge, in the buzzing of the bees; I shall be floating in the cloud that brings fertility, in the blowing wind, in the Crazy River, dearest; I shall be in every note of the earth.

A pair of stock doves, flapping their wings silently, landed by the canal to drink. When they saw me, they flurried away noisily. Suddenly I came to myself, as if awakening from a malarial sleep.

I returned to the hut to see Kolo and her kids . . . none of them was in sight. The others were grazing by the Crazy River, but the kolos were not among them.

I asked Uncle Husso. "I saw them in the cemetery," he told me, but they were not there either. I asked Uncle Cemo, Black Memosh, Crippled Hasso, Sister Hayganosh. I asked everyone I met. All of them had seen the kolos — in the walnut grove, at the fountainhead, in Mr. Asim's grape yard. I ran to every place they named. The kolos were not there; they had vanished.

In the evening, I watched for the flock to return to the village. I thought I saw Kolo in the cloud of dust rising from the slope in the distance. My heart beat crazily, and I threw myself into the flock. The kolos were not there.

I asked the shepherd. "I saw them," he said.

"They were at the peak of the mountain. Then I saw them on the other side of the river. I thought they had gone to drink water, so I sent the dogs, Blonde Girl and Half-Eared, to drive them back. The dogs returned howling . . ."

The Kolos and Three Springs

The poppies in the wheat fields had disappeared; the green almonds had hardened and their covers were no longer edible. One more spring was about to turn into summer.

Very early one morning, before dawn — I don't know how I woke up — I heard Kolo bleating. The sound was coming from just under my window. I dashed out of the house barefooted and in my underwear, but the sound had slipped down to the corporal's sour cherry orchard, and from there to the poplar grove. The wind absorbed half the sound. Then the bleating came from the cemetery, but I couldn't make myself go in that direction. Instead I ran toward Shako's hut.

The sound moved down the valley, to the river. I ran to the front of the hut, and from there I saw Kolo and her two kids under the sweet quince tree by the river. Stretching their long, slender necks, they raised their heads to the sky, as if they were trying to reach the misty leaves of the quince.

I reached the spot in a flash, but I couldn't see them anywhere. Suddenly I felt ice cold water lapping at my feet. Where the old quince leaned against it, a great rock had cracked into three pieces. Each crack had turned into a fountainhead that spurted streams of milklike foam.

Those three springs were in the exact spot where I saw the kolos for the last time, and I was the only one who witnessed their miracle.

The springs were discovered first by the goat kids, then by the red partridges. They came to drink water at every sunset. Later on, the spot became a resting place for the reapers who passed by on their way to and from their work. Those ice cold springs became the favorite place of the village children, and also of mine. We used to drink our fill from the Three Springs of Sweet Quince. Just like little kolos, lying on our stomachs with our faces right in the water.

The Dam

$\mathcal{U}$ntil I graduated from the university, I used to spend some part of my summer holidays in the village. I had lost my father long ago, and my mother had moved to the city.

One summer, for many reasons, I stayed in the village for a long time. Everything there seemed to have worn out, to have grown old and lost its shining colors. Three Springs had become three weak water cords, and even the Crazy River had stopped roaring.

Half of the juniper tree at Purple Rock had disappeared. It had rotted away.

In and around the village there were plenty of engineers and workers, carrying tape measures and binoculars, measuring everything and even counting the trees one by one. On the hills and in the valleys, giant yellow vehicles were digging the earth, loading and carrying it away. They were melting the mountains and the hills; they were changing the riverbeds.

All that tumult was for one thing: the building of a great dam about a hundred kilometers from the village. But the lake that the dam would create might extend up to our village and even flood it. They said so.

All the houses, all the fields and almond trees, that had belonged to the villagers had been confiscated and bought by "Father State." Some, those who had received their money, had left the village, but the majority were still there. In the evenings they gathered together in the village square, where they brooded over their fate. Mr. Asim, Black Memosh, Corporal Memet, and Uncle Cemo had long since died and become one with the earth. Those who gathered in the square were their children and their grandchildren.

One day the village headman said to them: "Mister Governor said that when the dam is completed, they are going to give electricity to all villages around." The villagers' hearts were torn by grief, their eyes were filled with tears, and they remained silent. What would they do with electricity when their village was under water?

At last the gendarmes brought the fatal message: The shutters of the dam had been closed. The peasants had to leave. Yet no one heeded that message. No one wanted to leave the village while his house and garden were still safe and dry. Perhaps no one believed it would happen.

But one month later, the roaring of the Crazy River was reduced to nothing in the lake that was swelling more and more each day. Slowly all the streams flowing into the Crazy River died away. The lake climbed the slopes, swallowing the Three Springs of the Sweet Quince. All the almond trees on the hillsides gradually disappeared in the water. Then the lake reached the fields and the first row of houses.

Although they had been warned, the peasants had

planted their gardens with melons again. When they saw the lake swallowing their work and their homes right under their noses, they seemed stricken by the goblins. Still, the lake blindly and disgracefully continued to creep upward. One more bit of life was buried with every bit of time that passed, buried at the bottom of the lake.

Uncle Cemo's grandson, trying to cut down his almond trees for firewood, got stuck in the muddy water and drowned. The young gendarme who struggled to rescue him drowned too, just a few weeks before he was to be discharged.

Until that event, the peasants had kept cool heads, but now they were in a sudden flurry. Fear and panic spread throughout the village. Water broke into anthills, into the nest of red partridges, into the pits of snakes, into the caves of wolves. It frightened the ants, the birds, the snakes, the wolves, the scorpions, the mole-crickets, the swarms of bees and grasshoppers out. Snakes crossed the village square in broad daylight. In the evenings, the endless howling of the wolves and jackals scared the life out of women and children. Still the lake rose, swallowing everything, driving all the living creatures and human beings away.

The water covered the minaret of the mosque and stopped at last at the foot of Purple Rock. Half of the bending juniper tree went under water; the other half remained on land. Who knows whether Sister Shako's kerchief was in the water or on the land?

No longer did the bleating of a kid, the song of a red partridge, or the screams of children echo beside the Crazy River. All that was left was a dirty, muddy lake with swarms of dead ants and grasshoppers, huge thistles, and swollen corpses of animals floating on the surface.

Life a thousand years old, hundreds of thousands of years old, melon gardens recently planted, almond trees loaded with fruit, tremendous walnut trees — all vanished in one season, unable to reach another autumn. The great story of life and of our village disappeared in the water of the lake. Who will believe me if I say: "Right there, under the muddy water at the height of a minaret, is the village where I was born and the hut that belonged to Shako and Kolo . . ." Who would believe that once there was a village here?

Only its song remains, echoing through the valleys and back from the hillsides:

90

There is no quince, no pear is left,
I can not know how they would taste.
Do not ask me for I will cry,
The village there, what was its name?

After Forty Years

Almost forty springs have passed since those days. No one has ever seen the little kolos again. As for me, wherever I see children, I see the little kolos next to them. When my daughter was born, I saw "Kolofosh." When my son was born, I saw "Kololo." I understand now that the little kolos are children of mine, of my country — they are the children of the whole world.

Almost forty autumns have passed since those

days. No one has seen Sister Shako or Kolo again. As for me, I know now that Sister Shako and Kolo are my mothers, and the mothers of my children, and of my wife. They are the mothers of my country. They are the mothers of the whole world.

That is all . . .

Once there was, once there wasn't, once there was a village by the Crazy River where Sister Shako and her goat Kolo lived . . .

Translator's Note

Some years ago, when I first read this book in its original Turkish, I was not only fascinated but deeply shaken by its plain, nearly wild story. The people seemed familiar to me, totally realistic. Yet the story was full of fantasy and poetry, and even though it's a sad tale, it holds much humor.

Everything about this book was special: the loving narration, the regional words, idioms, sayings, and traditions of eastern Turkey, where the author was born. Almost all the names in this book are in the diminutive form, so they all end with an "o" or "sh," which is characteristic of the region.

Dalokay followed no particular chronological order in his narrative; instead he followed his childhood memories, jumping back and forth, natural, sincere, and vivid. For this American edition, a few of the more jarring jumps have been reordered for ease of understanding.

After I read *Kolo*, as the book was originally called, I couldn't resist calling Vedat Dalokay to ask his permission to translate it. He was an old acquaintance of mine — a well-known architect who had once been the mayor of Ankara. But I had never known that he was also a very fine writer. His book was a great surprise for me and for everyone in my country who read it. It won several literary awards, including "The Best Storybook of the Year 1980" for adult literature. It was obvious that, like me, even the grown-ups could not help loving Kolo.

In the spring of 1991, before I finished translating the book into English, we lost Vedat Dalokay, together with his family, in a car accident. Now the book means even more to me than it did before. Not only was it a pleasure to translate, it was a duty to convey his marvelous story, so full of love, so warm and sensitive, to the children of the world, as he intended.

I want to thank Virginia Allen Jensen for her great help and efforts to bring this beautiful book to the United States.

GÜNER ENER, ISTANBUL, 1994